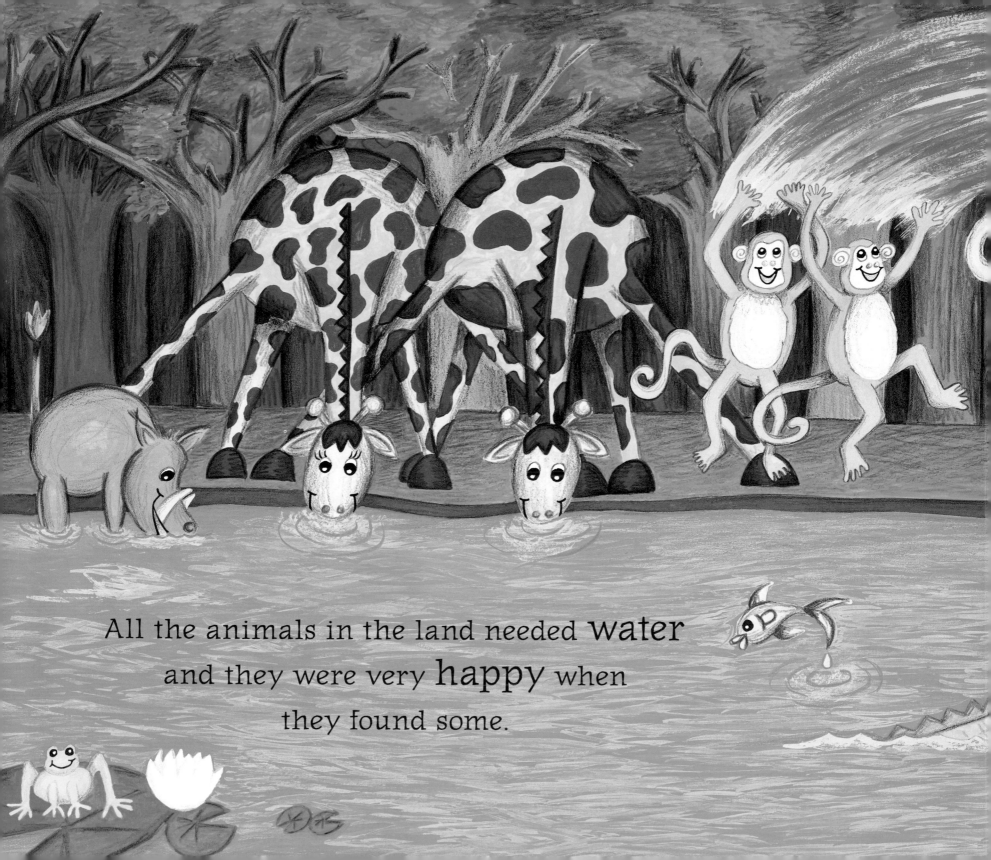

All the animals in the land needed water
and they were very happy when
they found some.

One pool of water was guarded by a **cheeky** baboon who told all the animals that it was his water. He did not allow the other animals to take even one sip from this pool.

One day, when the sun was very fierce, a Zebra was searching
for a drink because he was so hot and thirsty.
Now in those days of long ago,
the Zebra wore a coat of pure white fur.

The white-coated Zebra searched everywhere
and eventually he found the pool.
He was so happy, at last he could have a drink!

He raced down to the cool blue pool
and began to quench his thirst.

Just then the angry
baboon barked,

"GO AWAY!

This is my pool
and no one else can
drink this water."

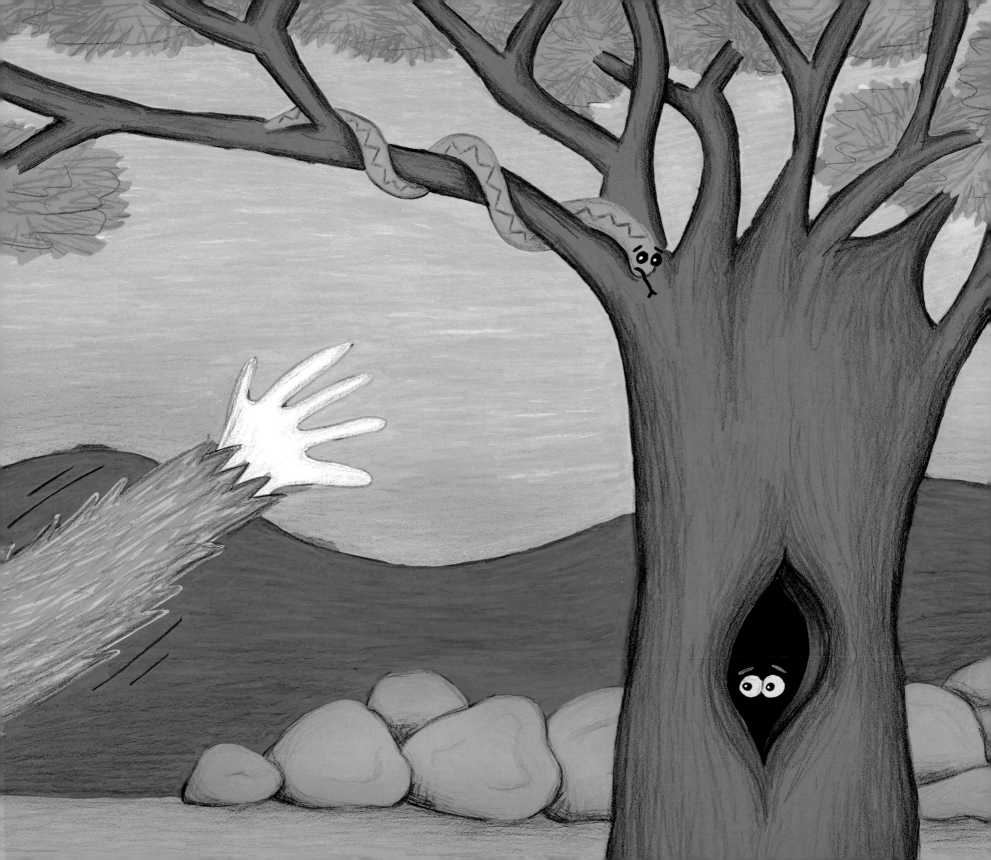

"But this water belongs to all of us"
answered the Zebra as he looked up
to find the baboon sitting
under a tree, roasting
a mealie on a fire.

This made the baboon even more angry.
He opened his mouth wide to show his sharp fangs
and he shouted,
"If you want water -
you must FIGHT for it!"

The Zebra did not want to fight,
but because he was so thirsty, the battle began.

Then suddenly, with a mighty kick
of the Zebra's back legs,

the baboon went flying high into the rocky field behind them.

The cheeky baboon
landed smack on his bottom,
and ever since that day you can still see the
bare, red patch where he landed.

The Zebra was also not so lucky...

With the force of his kick,
he stumbled backwards right
into the baboon's fire.
The hot sticks burnt black stripes
across his beautiful white fur.

The Zebra managed to get up out
of the fire, but when he saw all the
black stripes across his body he got such
a **fright** that he galloped back home as
fast as he could.

From that day on, zebras were born
with **black** stripes across their white fur.
They have come to love their special black and
white coats... but they're still not very fond of baboons.

Published in South Africa by Art Publishers (Pty) Ltd
Reg. No 1947/027008/07
PO Box 334, Howard Place, Cape Town, 7045, South Africa
Tel: +27 21 532 3020
www.artpublishers.co.za

First Published 2009
Second Revised Edition 2015